"*My Name is Erin: One Girl's Journey to Disc[...]*
think about my role in today's culture. It help[...]
created men and women differently for differ[...]
that God's way is perfect and His plan for wo[...]

"Erin's book is really great! Although written from the perspective of a tomboy, the truths in it apply to even a girly-girl like me. The book helped me understand God's call on my life as a girl."—Maddie

"I am so grateful to Erin Davis for writing this book! She presents key issues that young girls face and wonderfully shows how God's way is the best way. Finally, a book that takes big issues of faith and presents them in a relatable way to young girls. I love how she integrates God's Word throughout, showing girls how God's Word can be applied to everyday circumstances. This book has made a significant impact on my daughter!"—Michele, mom

my name is

ERIN

One Girl's Journey to
Discover Who She Is

Erin Davis

MOODY PUBLISHERS
CHICAGO

All Scripture quotations, unless otherwise indicated, are taken from *The Holy Bible, English Standard Version.* Copyright © 2000, 2001 by Crossway Bibles, a division of Good News Publishers. Used by permission. All rights reserved.

Scripture quotations marked ASV are taken from *The American Standard Version*, 1901, public domain.

Scripture quotations marked NIV are taken from the Holy Bible, New International Version®, NIV®. Copyright © 1973, 1978, 1984 by Biblica, Inc.™ Used by permission of Zondervan. All rights reserved worldwide. www.zondervan.com

All websites and phone numbers listed herein are accurate at the time of publication, but may change in the future or cease to exist. The listing of website references and resources does not imply publisher endorsement of the site's entire contents. Groups and organizations are listed for informational purposes, and listing does not imply publisher endorsement of their activities.

Edited by Annette LaPlaca
Interior and Cover design: Julia Ryan / www.DesignByJulia.com
Cover images: Shutterstock.com/Elise Gravel. Illustration of author: Julia Ryan
Interior images: Various artists/Shutterstock: borders, arrows, rainbow, crown, tree, perfume, necklace, flowers, faces, bullhorn, bee, sun, words. Chapter illustration: Beastfromeast/iStock
Author photo: Sarah Carter Photography

Library of Congress Cataloging-in-Publication Data

Davis, Erin, 1980-
  My name is Erin : one girl's journey to discover who she is / Erin Davis.
     pages cm
  Includes bibliographical references.
  ISBN 978-0-8024-0643-9
  1. Women--Religious aspects--Christianity--Juvenile literature. 2. Identity (Psychology)--Religious aspects--Christianity--Juvenile literature. 3. Preteens--Religioous life--Juvenile literature. 4. Teenage girls--Religious life--Juvenile literature. I. Title.
  BT704.D38 2013
  248.8'33--dc23
                    2013013125

We hope you enjoy this book from Moody Publishers. Our goal is to provide high-quality, thought-provoking books and products that connect truth to your real needs and challenges. For more information on other books and products written and produced from a biblical perspective, go to www.moodypublishers.com or write to:

Moody Publishers
820 N. LaSalle Boulevard
Chicago, IL 60610

1 3 5 7 9 10 8 6 4 2

Printed in the United States of America

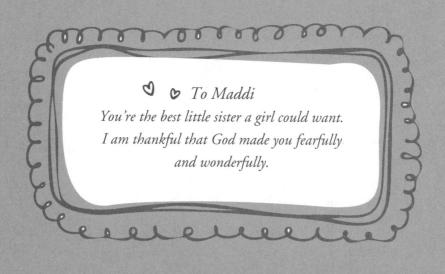

♡ ♡ To Maddi
You're the best little sister a girl could want.
I am thankful that God made you fearfully
and wonderfully.

Contents

CHAPTER 1

Girlhood 101: What's the Big Deal about Gender?

My name is Erin. That's me about the time my bangs hit their peak, circa seventh grade.

I have a serious aversion to shopping malls, I'm not a huge fan of pink, and my hair has been in a messy ponytail for 364 of the last 365 days. (I just cannot get the hang of flat irons, curling irons, or hairspray!) I spend a lot more time being loud and rowdy than I do being "gentle and quiet." My fingernails haven't been painted since my wedding, more than a decade ago. Don't get me wrong: I love being a girl. But if you're searching for the poster child for girly girlness, I'm afraid you'll need to keep looking.

I suppose that makes me a strange choice to write a book on God's Truth about being a girl. I mean, don't the women in the Bible love to cook and clean and wear flowing skirts in fields of flowers? Not exactly. At least, not all of them. In fact, as we look to the Bible for answers about what it means to be a girl, we will find women who were feisty, strong, and brave, as well as some women who used their gentle femininity for God's glory. From clever heroines to bold military leaders, these ladies can join me in the "We're Not Girly Girls" Club. I'll go ahead and sign you up for your free membership too, because whether you're a mega tomboy, a pretty-pretty princess, or someone somewhere in between, God has a plan for your girlhood that goes way beyond ribbons and curls.

Before we can get to the "what" of God's plan for us as girls we need to answer "why?" Why does it matter that God created men and women? Why did God make guys and girls so different? Why does gender (that's just a fancy word for the traits that make girls *girls* and boys *boys*) matter anyway?

Yep, you're a girl, but how does that fit into who you are as a daughter, sister, student, friend, athlete, dreamer, or future rock star? How does it impact how you live out your faith?

Great questions! I'm glad you asked.

I don't have it all figured out and I can't promise to answer every question about gender within the pages of this book, but I do know what it's like to wonder, "What kind of girl does God want me to be?" That question sent me running to the Bible for answers. What I found made me so excited to be a girl.

✿ A New Pair of Glasses

I've seen what can happen when we let the world tell us what gender means. It isn't pretty! I've counseled many girls who feel like the rope in a tug of war because they're torn between the messages of the culture and what they think a good, Christian girl should want to be like. I've *been* the girl who wondered if I could ever measure up to the women in the Bible without having a total personality transplant.

If you read the first book in this series, *My Name Is Erin: One Girl's Journey to Discover Truth*, you know that I've learned God's Word is like a pair of glasses that can change how we see the world. His Truth has certainly changed how I see gender. But it's not my mission to tell you how you should think about what it means to be a girl. Instead, I want to show you how to discover God's Truth for yourself.

꒰꒱ My name is Erin, and this is my story. ꒰꒱

🌼 A World without Pink and Blue

Here are a few of the ways gender has made headlines recently.

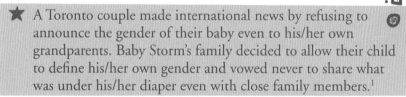

★ A Toronto couple made international news by refusing to announce the gender of their baby even to his/her own grandparents. Baby Storm's family decided to allow their child to define his/her own gender and vowed never to share what was under his/her diaper even with close family members.[1]

★ For the first time ever, the United States Navy decided to allow two women to share the traditional homecoming kiss upon the return of a Navy vessel.[2]

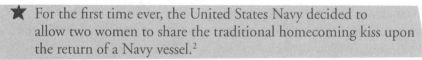

★ Several preschools made the news by banning all mentions of gender among even the youngest of students. Such schools have banned words like "him," "her," "he," and "she," and have invented new words to take their place.[3]

These stories got people talking. To be honest, they got folks fighting plenty too. Some people think we should simply erase gender from the world. No more blue is for boys and pink is for girls. Instead we should live in a genderless society where all the lines are blurred. Others think traditional gender lines must be protected or chaos will ensue. And there are plenty of people somewhere in the middle asking, "Why should I care about gender?"

❀ What's the Big Deal?

I can see why the young women in my world struggle to understand what it means to be a girl.

Every day I meet girls who do not know who God has made them to be or how God has called them to live. The consequences are devastating. Here are a few statements I've heard from girls recently:

🦋 "Every girl wants a real nice relationship and to be taken care of and to be loved . . . Since girls want this, why wouldn't I want to be in a romantic relationship with a girl because I want this too! All boys want is trouble."

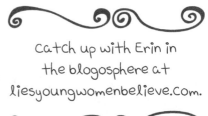

Catch up with Erin in the blogosphere at liesyoungwomenbelieve.com.

🐝 "I've been struggling with this question for quite a few weeks now . . . What's the purpose of marriage? That may seem like a dumb question, but God doesn't want our devotion and love to be divided. Isn't that exactly what happens when you marry and eventually have kids?"

🐝 "I think we hold up this Proverbs 31 woman way too high on some pedestal, and the end result is a lot of frustration, guilt, and shame because we as women can never measure up. I hate to say it, but women need to stop living in her shadow. We are not created to serve or be slaves to men."

These girls don't understand that the differences between guys and girls are a good thing! Because they don't understand the way God wired boys, they assume that boys only want trouble. Because they don't understand the roles girls are designed for, they struggle to find purpose. Because they don't know the reasons God made

13

Proverbs 31 is a passage that describes a version of Superwoman. She's a wife, mom, seamstress, chef, real estate tycoon, and fashonista. Many Christians hold her up as the "perfect woman." This passage was actually written as a description of a good woman by a mother to her son (Proverbs 31:1), not as an actual billboard for what we should all look like.

gender in the first place, they have a hard time making sense of their relationships, their feelings, and their future.

They are not alone. This is a great place for me to introduce a group of girls I just know you'll love. I really wanted to get into the minds of the readers of this book. I'm a little older than you (ahem, maybe a lot older!), and I would never assume to have you all figured out. So some friends and I hit the road to hang out

The Gab Gallery

with young women across the country and get their take on what it means to be a girl. The girls we talked to were probably a lot like your group of friends. They were mostly Christians (many were raised in church), but like me they had big questions about what kind of girl God wants them to be. You'll hear their take on gender throughout this book.

These girls love to talk! That's why I like to call them the Gab Gallery. From here on out, I'll just call them "the Gallery." It's their job to make you feel that you are a part of a conversation about what it means to be a girl (because you are!). If you love to talk, you'll fit right in.

If the Gallery were teaching Girlhood 101, here's a peek into their lesson plans.

★ "I do not like it when I am called 'a young woman' . . . I'm not in to that whole etiquette thing."

★ "Women stay home . . . sometimes, and men go to work and pay the bills. Sometimes women work, but mostly men work and mow the lawn. Except at my house."

★ "Guys are easier; they are more fun. Girls make such a big deal about things!"

Girls in high school in the 1950s had to watch "Mental Hygiene" films that promoted good manners in all situations.[4] I'm guessing those movies weren't exactly action-packed!

There's nothing exactly wrong with the way the Gallery was trying to define the differences between girls and guys, but their ideas were kind of all-over-the-map. One girl said she didn't like the whole "etiquette thing" (she later told us she did not like to be called a "lady." Noted!). Rewind to the 1950s when having good manners was a huge part of being a girl. Can a modern girl resist all that lady talk and still be feminine? Still be girly?

Another girl said women stay home while men work and mow the lawn. That throws us back to some very traditional gender roles that may leave you feeling like you're being pulled into an episode of *Leave It to Beaver*. But even she admitted that wasn't how things really worked at her own house. Maybe there is no normal. Should there be?

That last girl painted guys and girls with a really wide brush. Guys are easy and fun; girls are dramatic. I'm guessing she has some girl drama in her life! Are guys really just cavemen who think simple thoughts and like to have fun? And are all girls drama queens? Did God make us to be that way?

My goodness! If we think of studying God's plan for being a girl like unraveling a knot of mixed messages, we seem to be tying the knot more tightly by stirring up more questions than answers. As I listen to what the Gallery is saying and line it up with my own heart, it becomes very clear that most of us are fairly confused about what it means to be a girl.

✿ Hop into the Wayback Machine

How did we get here? Let's have a brief history lesson. (Don't worry, there won't be a quiz.)

In the 1950s being a girl meant dresses and dreams of a future dream house, complete with white picket fence, where your 2.5 children could play.[5]

In the 1960s a movement called "feminism" caught fire in America. (Speaking of catching fire, this is an era when women burned their bras in the name of change. Weird!) Women were supposed to be strong, loud, and take-charge. They ditched feminine touches like dresses, pink, and frills as they marched.[6] In the 1980s girls just wanted to have fun, at least that's what pop singer Cyndi Lauper told us. There are plenty of fashion trends from the eighties that are simply too gaudy to mention here (I'm talking to you, shoulder pads!), but one trend worth noting is power dressing. Women in the workforce were the norm in the eighties, and they wanted to show they were equal to (or better than) their male coworkers. So women rocked suits and big hair with the occasional touch of blue eye shadow.[7] An eighties

It didn't feel like the fairy tale I was promised it would be!

girl had her sights set on a corner office. I was in junior high and high school in the nineties. The clearest message I heard was that anything guys could do, I could do better. I also learned to put all my hopes for a happy life into the basket of an important career. At the dawn of the new millennium, I had it all: high-paced career, fancy degrees in frames on the wall, and a hubby who was happy to let me run the show. But it didn't feel like the fairy tale I was promised it would be. I couldn't shake my craving for more.

17

If we look at history like a map, the girls of past decades point us to the spot that says, "You are here." What does it mean to be a girl right now?

Is a modern girl powerful or soft? Does she want a career or a family? Does she deserve to be taken care of or want to be in charge? How can we look beyond the messages of the fashion industry and pop singers and figure out what God would say if He were teaching *Girlhood 101*?

It is possible to know God's plan for gender, but before we get there let's pull out our magnifying glasses and look just a little closer at what's on the line.

Here is what researchers are saying about you:

★ For the first time ever, more of you are saying "I don't" to the idea of marriage.

★ Living with a guy you're not married to is okay with you.[8]

★ For the first time ever, women are earning the majority of college degrees. You want to finish your education. You want a career. And you want at least as much responsibility in your job as the guys you know.[9]

★ Most of you aren't sure if motherhood is for you, or you want to delay it until after you've accomplished your career goals.

★ If you become moms, you don't feel pressure to work less to raise kids. You want to have it all.[10]

Some researchers have said that marriage and family are still important goals for girls your age, but you're not sure if and why it matters.[11] (Hint: it does!)

Some of you may read that list and think, "That sounds about right." Others may look at that list and think, "No way! That's not how I think."

Some of you may be straddling the fence. No matter where you land, lean in and listen closely. It's less important for us to figure out exactly what we think about being a girl and more important for us to ask God to show us His heart for gender.

The bottom line is that we cannot simply erase gender from our lives. We cannot delete words like "he" and "she" from our vocabulary without new words with the same meaning creeping into our conversations. Nope, boys and girls are here to stay, and so are our differences. Our best bet is to seek to understand those differences through the lens of God's Truth!

which brings me to the
first girl who ever lived

CHAPTER 2

Who Do I Look Like? Checking Out the Role of Image-Bearer

have two sons. Eli is my firstborn. Every inch of him—from the top of his head to the bottom of his feet—looks just like his daddy. If he hadn't been in my tummy for nine months, I'd be tempted to think he was just a clone, created in some weird science lab.

Noble is my second-born, and I don't think he got a single cell of his dad's DNA. Everything about him looks like me. If I were two years old with short hair and a Thomas-the-Train shirt on, you'd think we were twins. But that would be weird . . .

Who do you look like?

Do you have your mother's eyes and your dad's freckled nose? Do people always compare you to someone else's baby pictures or tell you, "You look just like so-and-so?"

I've always thought God made us look like the members of our family so we knew where we belonged. Gender is like that. When we turn to God's Word to see why He made men and women in the first place, we find that gender is not really about what makes us different as much as it's about showing us who our true family is.

The Bible opens with these words: "In the beginning, God created the heavens and the earth" (Genesis 1:1).

Before anything you've ever touched, tasted, seen, heard, or smelled existed, there was God. Genesis 1 is the thrilling account of how He spoke everything into existence. One minute there was darkness; the next there was light. One day there was empty space; the next there was land.

Everything written about in Genesis 1—from plants to stars to great sea creatures—was created on purpose. Keep that in mind as we peek in on the story. About the time the birds start singing and the sea teems with fish, God shifts gears and does something very different: "So God created man in his own image, in the image of God he created him; male and female he created them" (Genesis 1:27).

"In the beginning, God created the heavens and the earth" (Genesis 1:1).

That's just one short, little verse, but it's loaded with Truth about gender. Rapid fire, here are the three big takeaways.

1. God created men and women.

2. God created men and women in His image.

3. God created men and women as distinctly different from the very beginning.

Let's peel back the layers and see why each of these pieces of the gender puzzle matters so much.

Created On Purpose

God created men and women. That may feel like a no-brainer, but think about that fact for a minute. Let it marinate.

Since God is the Creator of gender, shouldn't *He* get to decide what that looks like? Hollywood didn't create men and women. Why should they get to tell us what it means to be a girl? Fashion magazines can only photograph what God made. That's not nearly the same as creating it from scratch. Your peers may have an idea of what kind of girl you should be, but they were created by God just like you are. Should they really be calling the shots? Catch my drift?

I totally plagiarized that whole potter/clay analogy. Here it is again straight from God's Word: "You turn things upside down, as if the potter were thought to be like the clay! Shall what is formed say to the one who formed it, 'You did not make me'? Can the pot say to the potter, 'You know nothing'?" (Isaiah 29:16 NIV).

God made men and women, which gives Him the unique ability to decide what we should be like. Because He is the Creator and we are the created, we need to look to Him for answers about what it means to be a girl.

Let's think of it a different way. Imagine you are a lump of clay. You're not sure what you are supposed to be beyond that. Should you try to flatten yourself into a plate? Should you work to stretch yourself tall like a vase? Will you always be just a lump?

The best way to answer these questions is not to turn and talk to the other lumps of clay. They're in the same boat as you! Instead, your questions must be answered by the Potter. He's the one who knows what you should be, and He's the only one capable of shaping you into what you were made for. (Whoever heard of a lump of clay sculpting itself?)

Would you stop reading for a minute and just pray a simple prayer with me?

God, You created me. Would You show me Your design for what it means to be a girl?

✿ Created as Image Bearers

Remember how I told you that gender works to show us where we belong? Go back to Genesis 1:27 and you'll see what I mean: "So God created man in his own image, in the image of God he created him; male and female he created them" (emphasis addded). Did you notice how the record skips there for a second? "So God created man in his own image." Repeat. "In the image of God he created him."

In the image of God he created him.

If we hop back a verse, we find this same idea presented in a conversation: "Then God said, 'Let us make man in our image, after our likeness. And let them have dominion over the fish of the sea and over the birds of the heavens and over the livestock and over all the earth and over every creeping thing that creeps on the earth'" (Genesis 1:26, emphasis added).

Who is God talking to? Himself actually! God the Father, God the Son, and God the Holy Spirit were present at creation, and they were talking about you. Well, not *you* exactly, but they were brainstorming about creating something totally different from the birds of the air and the beasts of the field.

From the moment He first spoke of making man (as in *humankind*), God mentioned making us to be like Him. He repeated that idea twice more in the next couple of sentences.

Put on your listening ears, ladies. This is the most important lesson there is about gender: The purpose of your gender is to reflect who God is. Since God doesn't seem to mind repeating Himself, I'll take my cue from Him.

The reason girls are girls and guys are guys is to reveal something about God!

In Isaiah 43 God is talking about gathering His children when He says, "Everyone who is called by my name, whom I created for my glory, whom I formed and made" (Isaiah 43:17, emphasis added).

Don't miss this! The secret to your purpose is right there, staring at you from the first few pages of the Bible. God says it over and over in verses like Isaiah 43:17. You were made to bring God glory. The purpose of your design is to point to Him.

Understanding your unique role as a girl isn't really about being a certain kind of girl. It isn't about rules. It's not about a profile. It's about putting God on display.

❀ Different Is Good

Think back to first-grade Sunday school, and you might recall a little more detail about creation than we pick up in Genesis 1:26–27. Those verses give us the bottom line. They're like the Wikipedia version. Summary: God created men and women in His image.

It's enough to help you pass a test, but it doesn't fill in much detail.

In Genesis 2 we read the rest of the story. God formed the man out of dust and breathed life into his nostrils. God gave the man his very own farm called the garden of Eden. God named the man *Adam*, and it didn't take long for Adam to feel lonely, so God made a woman to help him. God seems to love a good Hallmark-card moment as much as the rest of us, so God formed the woman out of the man's ribs, prompting Adam to exclaim, "This at last is bone of my bones and flesh of my flesh; she shall be called Woman, because she was taken out of Man" (Genesis 2:23).

We have no reason to think that Adam had been in the garden very long without his lady, but it must have felt otherwise because the first time he saw her Adam exclaimed, "At last!" All that "bone of my bones" and "flesh of my flesh" stuff doesn't really make my heart pitter-patter, but it seemed to work for Eve. And just like that, the very first man and woman were made. And they were different from each other from the very beginning.

God could have created anything He wanted to in that garden. He had already spoken the planets into existence and made light and darkness by saying the word. He made Adam out of a sand sculpture. His ability to create was not limited in any way by anything.

When Adam looked around and saw that there was no one like him, God could have squeezed together a little more dirt and made a second Adam or a Bill or a Tom or a Brad. Surely Adam would have felt less lonely if he had his own football team to entertain him.

But God chose not to make someone exactly like the man. Instead, He made something similar but very different. Sure, we know now that men and women are necessary for procreation (That's a fancy word for making babies!), but it didn't have to be that way. God could have organized things so that babies were delivered by storks if He'd wanted to.

Surely baby-making wasn't the only reason God made two people who were so different. If the purpose of our gender is to put God on display, is it possible that who you are as a girl shows off something different about Him from what your dad or brothers ever can?

God's Truth says, "In the image of God he created them." Both men and women are made to reflect the image of God. Guys and girls each reflect God in a unique and distinct way.

Those who want to scrub the world clean of gender differences seem to think that differences are a bad thing. Not true! God created men and women different on purpose and with His glory in mind.

God could have organized things so that babies were delivered by storks if He'd wanted to.

God Is Like . . .

Remember those girls in the Gallery? From Springfield to Little Rock, big city to small town, they all admired women in their lives for the same reasons. Whether it was a grandma or a best friend's mom, they were drawn to women who were faithful, kind, loving, and interested in building strong relationships with the people around them.

Did you know that the very qualities they admire in the women they know are used to describe God in His Word? Now we are getting somewhere!

★ Faithful

Faithful means true-blue loyal, with steadfast affection that never gives up. The Psalms say, "Your steadfast love, O Lord, extends to the heavens, your faithfulness to the clouds" (Psalm 36:5) and "You are mighty, O Lord, and your faithfulness surrounds you" (Psalm 89:8 NIV).

★ Kind

Kind means sympathetic and warm-hearted, with actions that measure up to the feelings. God's Word calls God "kind": "I will tell of the kindnesses of the Lord" (Isaiah 63:7 NIV).

★ Loving

Everybody knows that true *loving* goes way beyond sweet words; how people act is what really shows true love. When the Bible describes God's love, it talks about His "ways" and deeds: "All the ways of the Lord are loving and faithful toward those who keep the demands of his covenant" (Psalm 25:10 NIV) and "Let the one who is wise heed these things and ponder the loving deeds of the Lord" (Psalm 107:43 NIV).

★ Relational

The entire Bible tells the story of how God is interested in building strong relationships. Remember the first time we heard God speak about creating men and women in Genesis 1:26–27? Right there, in the very beginning, we see that God is a *relational* God. God the Father, God the Son, and God the Holy Spirit relate to each other and communicate with each other. God values relationships!

The rest of the Bible is all about God's efforts to have a strong, loving relationship with His people. These are the very same qualities the Gallery said they admired most about the women they knew.

Now certainly, men can be faithful, kind, loving, and relational, but these things form the very essence of what it means to be a girl. Remember the purpose of our gender? It's to reveal something about God! The things that make you a girl, at your core—those things are designed to shine a white-hot spotlight on who God is. Cool, huh?

That's why being a godly girl isn't really about liking or hating pink. Instead of trying to figure out who we are and then trying to decide if that's okay with God, we need to flip the mirror outward.

Why don't you take a minute right now and write a letter to God telling Him what you love most about Him. Go ahead; write your answers on the next page. Then, ask Him to show you how you can use your gender to put Him on display.

CHAPTER 3

It's Good to
Be a Girl:
Thinking Beyond
Handbags and
Bubble Baths

I was the girls wrestling champion my eighth-grade year. We had a wrestling tournament in PE class. The winners kept advancing. I must have pinned a lot of girls to the mat because I ended up in the championship match, which happened to play out in the gym in front of the entire junior high.

I've always been a little scrappy.

Most people wouldn't list "good wrestler" among the characteristics of a godly girl. We are supposed to be lovers, not fighters. And yet here I am, a scrappy girl with a wrestling trophy in my closet.

The fact that I don't fit most lists of what a girl *should* be like has always caused me some angst. While my twin sister was playing house, I was pretending to be the boss. Other girls are so naturally sweet they come across like little cocker spaniels. I've always been a bit more like a bulldog. It's not that I'm masculine, but I've spent plenty of years wondering if it's okay to be me. Specifically, I longed to know if it was possible to be the kind of girl God wanted me to be if I had no desire to live in Barbie's dream house.

I was strong, but I heard that girls were the weaker sex.

I was loud and rowdy, but I read in the Bible that true beauty comes from a "gentle and quiet spirit" (1 Peter 3:4).

I wanted to be successful, but I wondered how I'd manage having a corner office and being a mom someday.

I wanted to be tough, but I was drawn to women who were soft and vulnerable.

I wanted to be me, but I couldn't shake the feeling that maybe being a boy was somehow . . . better.

I know I'm not the only one to feel this way. My friend Nancy Leigh DeMoss wrote about similar feelings in the book *Lies Young Women Believe.* "As a teenager, I had a strong desire to serve the Lord," Nancy wrote. "Somehow I developed the mindset that if I'd been a man, God could have used my life in a more significant way. I struggled to understand and accept God's calling for me as a woman."[12]

Nancy describes a struggle many girls face. The culture preaches that guys and girls should be the same in every area of life, and yet we are not the same. God made guys and girls distinctly different. (Remember: those differences are designed to put the unique qualities of God on display!)

As the world around us screams, "Be just like the boys!" our design yells back, "But God made me this way to show the world about Him!" Has this tug of war ever made you feel frustrated about being a girl? Like Nancy and I, have you ever wondered if being a boy would be so much . . . easier?

✿ I Enjoy Being a Girl

True. Being a girl isn't all "sugar and spice and everything nice." It can be tough, but that doesn't mean that being a girl is a bad thing. In fact, God calls it just the opposite. (We'll get to that soon.)

Before we dig up why God thinks girls are great, why don't you do some brainstorming yourself? What is it you love most about being a girl?

Go ahead and jot your answers down.

_____

_____

_____

_____

_____

_____

_____

_____

_____

_____

_____

_____

Did you list shopping? Manicures and pedicures? Friends? Did you write anything down about hair or makeup or shoes? I admit those are all pretty great perks of girlhood. The poor boys never have a good excuse to get their toes done or buy a pretty pair of shoes to put those toes in (aww . . .).

35

This conversation reminds me of the Rodgers and Hammerstein big musical number "I Enjoy Being a Girl." Just in case you're not a fan of musical theatre from the 1950s let me sum up the song for you.

The lyrics talk about everything there is to love about being a girl. Brand-new hairdos made the list. So do getting flowers from "a fella" and dresses made of lace. Things start to get kind of weird when the song mentions a girl talking on the telephone for hours with a pound and a half of cold cream on her face.

Obviously, the times have changed a bit. We may text for hours, but we aren't likely to be found gabbing for that long on the phone. And who uses cold cream any more? Our grandmas that's who!

I do love a brand-new hairdo, and nothing beats a spa night. But somehow I can't imagine these are the best things about girls in God's book.

❀ It Was Very Good

Let's go back to the very beginning, when God designed the very first girl. He didn't look at Eve and think, "Whoops! I guess I should have made her stronger." Or, "Poor thing, if she didn't love to talk so much, I could really use her for something big!" I also don't think God's intention was that Eve was only a pretty face, good for nothing but trips to the mall and spotting cute fig-leaf fashion when she saw it.

When God looked at Adam and Eve—two people who were similar but designed to reveal something different about God—He reached one conclusion: "And God saw everything that he had made, and behold it was very good" (Genesis 1:31).

When God made Earth, He said that it was good (Genesis 1:10). When He covered the earth with plants and fruit and trees, He said that it was good (Genesis 1:12). When God made the sun and the moon, He said that it was good (Genesis 1:18). When He made pelicans and whales and elephants and zebras, He said that it was good (Genesis 1:25).

It's better than good to be a girl. It's VERY good.

But when God made man and woman—two distinct image-bearers, each with a specific story to tell about God— He added an extra word. Your creation story isn't just *good*, it's *very good*. It's better than good to be a girl. It's *very* good.

It's not as if guys are the fancy sports car and girls are just the hood ornament. God didn't pour all the talent, gifts, strength, opportunities, and abilities into the mold for Adam and make Eve with the leftovers. Nope. The things that make you different from the guys around you are there by design because they reveal something unique about God.

We live in a culture that values strength, power, and an unwillingness to back down from battle. These are characteristics clearly seen in most men. They are also characteristics of God. God is strong! God is powerful! There is no battle too big for God. But these are not the only admirable qualities of God.

Let me introduce you to some girls whose stories I ripped right from the pages of the Bible. These ladies can tell us in their own words that it's good to be a girl, primarily because being a girl allows us to reflect a good

God! Notice that these are not cartoon characters who look perfect, act perfect, and ooze perfect womanhood. These are real girls. I don't know if they love pink or if they ever had their nails done. The inspired writers of the Bible failed to mention if any of these ladies like handbags, because that's not what matters most about living out God's design.

Part of the reason we struggle to embrace our design as girls is because the essence of being a girl often gets boiled down to some checklist of dos and don'ts. "A real girl is a bubbly, giggly shopaholic." That, my friends, is a straw man (er . . . I mean . . . straw woman). A straw man is a person set up to serve as a cover. They're designed to distract from the real deal. That's what happens when we try to look at being a girl as if there were some sort of formula or checklist we have to live by. At the risk of sounding a bit like a broken record, let me remind you that God made girls to reveal something about Him. No one ever made a complete and exhaustive checklist of what God is like. He's too complex for that! Since we are just mirrors of Him, no one will ever be able to say,

A girl needs to be just like this:

The ladies in the Bible who show us God's plan for womanhood are different from each other, just like the girls in the Gallery are different and you and I are different. Some are bold, and some are timid. Some were probably girly girls, and others might have preferred to jump in on a game of football. They're a great reminder that being God's girl is less about likes and dislikes and more about seeking to have a heart like God's.

38

🦋 Hannah: The Crier

I have a male friend who says that when girls get together, they're gonna cry. I have to admit I'm guilty as charged, especially if there is a good chick flick playing. We girls tend to be more emotional than our male counterparts. In fact, did you know that women cry an average of 5.3 times a month? Guys, on the other hand only boohoo about 1.4 times a month.[14] It's a scientific fact! Sometimes girls need to burst into tears.

Expressing our emotions easily and often is one of the trademarks of being a girl.

Hannah was a girl who wasn't afraid to shed a tear. In fact, in 1 Samuel 1:1–18 we find Hannah as an emotional wreck. She couldn't get pregnant, and she was dealing with some serious mean-girl stuff at the hands of her husband's other wife, Peninnah. So 1 Samuel 1:7 tells us, "Therefore Hannah wept and would not eat."

Ever have a cry so big that your stomach hurt? That's what happened to Hannah. Her emotions were so raw that she could barely function. Been there. Done that! In verses 10–11 the Bible says that Hannah wept bitterly and prayed an emotional prayer to the Lord.

Eli the priest was so taken aback by all the crying that he thought Hannah was drunk (1 Samuel 1:14). I suppose that when we get all worked up emotionally, maybe we can come across as a little out of control.

73% of the time when men cry, tears do not roll down their cheeks. They just get misty-eyed.

39

But God didn't freak out over Hannah's tears. He didn't try to shush her or drop a hint by humming, "Big Girls Don't Cry" (I'm not sure if God would hum; I'm just embellishing a bit). Instead, God responded to Hannah's emotional plea and gave her a son. She named him Samuel and later sent him to live in the temple out of gratitude that God heard her prayers (1 Samuel 21).

Did you know that God has emotions too? The Bible tells us that God gets . . .

★ *Angry* (Deuteronomy 1:37, Exodus 32:10)

★ *Distressed* (Isaiah 63:9)

★ *Grieved* (Ephesians 4:30)

★ *Pleased* (1 Kings 3:10)

★ *Glad* (Zephaniah 3:17)

★ *Moved to pity* (Judges 2:18)

God isn't a cartoon character either. He isn't one-dimensional, unable to feel and express a range of emotions. In fact, Genesis 6:6 tells us that the sin on the earth in the days of Noah "grieved him to his heart." God's heart can be broken too! In Jeremiah 48:31 God *wails* and *cries* over the sin of the people of Moab, which sounds a lot like Hannah's emotional outburst. John 11:35 records that "Jesus wept" when His friend Lazarus died.

We are designed to reflect God. Our emotions mirror His. I'm not saying God has mood swings or that we should express everything we feel and then claim, "I'm just being like God!" (Warning: Unless you like being grounded, do not try that excuse on your parents!) Our emotions are subject to sin, and God's are not. The Bible does warn us against the danger of expressing emotions without self-control (Proverbs 25:28), but the emotional side of you is good for more than just inducing chocolate cravings. Our emotions point to a God who is not an unfeeling robot. Nope! He feels and responds deeply.

🦋 Mary: The Huge Heart

In the Gospels we find two sisters with very different personalities. This leads to the occasional catfight between them, however it also shows that we can be unique in our girlhood and still showcase something big about God.

Mary shows God's ability to love deeply. Mary is most famous for what she did when Jesus came to visit her house: Nothing. Nada. Not a thing. While her sister Martha (we will get to her next) worked herself into a total tizzy with housework, Mary just sat at Jesus' feet and soaked up His presence (Luke 10:39).

Mary let her whole world stop because she loved Jesus so much. Girls love deeply. Certainly, guys are capable of deep love for others too, but it tends to be our default to love with our whole hearts.

John 11:32 describes how Jesus comes to Mary after her brother, Lazarus, died. Mary doesn't save face by trying to appear calm. She is not stoic. She falls down at Jesus' feet and pours out her grief to Him (John 11:32).

Mary felt the emotions of her brother's death very deeply, and she didn't try to put on a brave face and act like everything was okay.

41

I bet some of you are like Mary. There are people in your life that you love with your whole heart. You are highly sensitive to the ebb and flow of relationships. When something isn't right, you feel it deeply and express it dramatically.

God loves deeply too: "I pray that you, being rooted and established in love, may have power, together with all the Lord's holy people, to grasp how wide and long and high and *deep is the love of Christ*, and to know this love that surpasses knowledge—that you may be filled to the measure of all the fullness of God" (Ephesians 3:17–19 NIV, emphasis added).

When you love people with your whole heart, you are showing the world that God does the same.

❀ Martha: The Talker

Talking is one of my favorite pastimes. If I have a free afternoon, I'd prefer to spend it hanging out and talking with a friend (preferably over a caramel latte). I don't really even care what we're talking about; I just love the interaction that comes with a good talk.

Did you know that women use an average of 20,000 words per day? Men average only 7,000.[17]

Most girls have the gift of gab. Researchers have found that women talk three times as much as men.[16]

We girls also tend to use talking to help us think through our feelings and experiences. That's what Martha, Mary's sister, did. When Lazarus died she ran out to meet Jesus to talk about it (John 11:20–27).

Martha is most famous for what she said in response to Mary sitting at Jesus' feet (Luke 10:38–42). Martha shows us the danger of too many words when she comes out of the kitchen to give Jesus a piece of her mind for not asking her sister to do more housework. (Remember, Mary loved Jesus so deeply she stopped everything and sat at His feet.)

Martha felt stressed, ignored, and put upon—and she wanted to talk about those feelings.

Giving life to every emotion by talking about it is not the way of God. Certainly there are times when it is best to keep our mouths shut and push back against our tendency to want to talk *everything* through, but in both of these encounters Jesus was open to having a conversation with Martha. She talked, and He talked back. Throughout the entire Bible we find God talking to His people about what matters.

Isaiah 1:18 says, "Come now let us reason together, says the Lord." In other words, let's talk about it! God invites us into an ongoing conversation with Him through prayer, and He talks back through His Word and the promptings of the Holy Spirit. There are plenty of examples recorded in the Bible of God talking audibly to His people. He can do that anytime He wants to (He's God after all!). But He has given us His Word as a way to "talk" with us about what matters, and He invites us to talk to Him often about what's going on in our lives.

My husband, Jason, is a classic "man of few words." He doesn't talk much. Several years ago, I was feeling frustrated because I had so much to say and he had so little. Talking to someone who doesn't love to talk back is frustrating! I was praying about it one day and just felt the Lord say to my heart, "Use your words with Me." In other words, "Talk to Me."

So I started talking to God more often. I worried less about saying the right words or getting to my point in as few words as possible. I simply started talking to God. How awesome is it that we love a God who wants us to talk to Him?

"Do not be anxious about anything, but in everything by prayer and supplication with thanksgiving let your requests be made known to God"
Philippians 4:6.

What percentage of your 20,000 words do you use with God? Does He just get one or two words a day, or are you talking to Him all day long about your life?

Martha wanted to talk about things, and that's okay. God invites us to talk to Him often.

The point is not that you have to be a Mary, a Martha, or a Hannah. There are no formulas for being a godly girl, but each of these women reveals something about God simply by being herself.

Here's the bigger lesson: The best way to learn who you should be is to study who God is. You are an image-bearer, made to show the world something unique about the character of God.

We tend to get it backward. We size ourselves up and wonder, "Is this who God made me to be?" Instead we should seek to be more like Him and ask, "Does who I am show others who God is?"

Ephesians 5:1 says, "Therefore be imitators of God, as beloved children."

God made you a girl on purpose and for a purpose. Your job is to reflect Him.

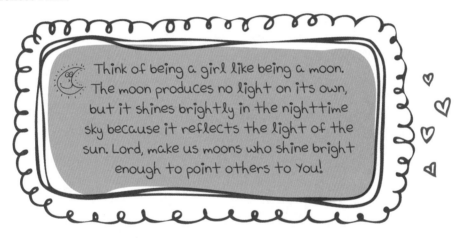

Think of being a girl like being a moon. The moon produces no light on its own, but it shines brightly in the nighttime sky because it reflects the light of the sun. Lord, make us moons who shine bright enough to point others to You!

If we want to be God's girls, we need to work to discover who He is, what His heart is passionate about, and what He wants the world to see when they look at Him, and work to reveal those things to others.

CHAPTER 4

Twisted:
What Being a Girl DOESN'T Mean

Being a girl may be "very good," but that doesn't mean it's always very easy. Part of my journey to discover my purpose on the planet has been wrestling with the ways being a girl is difficult. We aren't princesses locked up in some luxurious castle. Our reality is harsher than endless bubble baths and pedicures. There are parts of living out God's design that are really tough! I'm not just talking about dealing with hormones here (though that can be a doozy!). I'm talking about a way of living that forces us to swim upstream.

Culture tends to push back against the idea that guys and girls have different roles to play. The world tells us we can simply ignore what the Bible says, but I've never had much luck at making tough things go away simply because I ignored them. Have you?

Some folks are turning their backs on God's plan for girls, while others seem to want to turn God's design into a contest about who holds the most power. This makes it even more difficult for us to understand who God made us to be.

Have you gotten the impression that a woman's role in God's kingdom is to work in the nursery and bake a pie for every church function? Maybe, like my friend Nancy, who thought "significant" ministry was only for men, you've felt like all the top jobs on the ministry totem pole are reserved for men and you're stuck at the bottom with the not-so-exciting leftovers.

Does it seem like the ladies who are really committed to God's plan for womanhood have checked their talents, personality, and spunk at the door of the church? Do they seem like doormats to you? (Psst! A doormat is someone who gets stepped on—a lot! It's someone who lets everyone else walk all over her.)

I've had those feelings too, but what matters most is how God feels. Let me assure you God's plan is not to assign you boring and trivial work for His kingdom. He did not make you to be a doormat.

But don't take my word for it. As you seek to discover your own purpose, run hard toward the Word of God! Take what you think you know about God's design for girls and squeeze it through the filter of what the Bible says.

It's Time for a Checkup

Before we roll up our sleeves and dig into God's Word, can I encourage you to do a quick heart checkup? In my own life, I have found that the verses we are going to look at next make my back arch and my toes feel a little bruised. (Hint: This girls wrestling champion is going to step into the ring with *submission*. Join me!)

Psst! The Bible says there is no ministry totem pole. Check out 1 Corinthians 12:12-31. ♡

48

I don't like to think about anyone being in charge of me—except me. I don't like the idea that I can't have total control. But the root of those feelings is buried in my own heart. God and His Word are not the problem.

Think back to when you were a little girl, around the age of two or three. Can you remember what your favorite toy was? Mine was a homely little doll named "Baby Beans." Whether your favorite toddler possession was a baby doll or a blankie, I am sure you used one word to describe it: "Mine!" All toddlers do it. They take possessions very seriously and guard their stuff as if it were worth a million bucks. But to those of us who are a little older, outbursts of "Mine! Mine! Mine!" just look silly. Kids can't buy toys; they've never worked a day in their lives. They can't properly care for a toy or fix it if it breaks. They are possessive of something they do not really possess.

That's how it is with us. We want to be in the driver's seat, but we're reading the wrong map. We want to be in charge, but we've forgotten we're just clay and God is the Potter.

Would you take a minute and tell God what worries you about surrendering to His plan for your design? Do you think He will ask you to be someone you don't like? Are you afraid you will have to submit to someone who will abuse you or treat you poorly? Is *submission* a scary word that makes you feel out of control?

Remember that one of the characteristics of God is that He wants to talk to us. So go ahead: Tell Him what kind of girl you don't want to be.

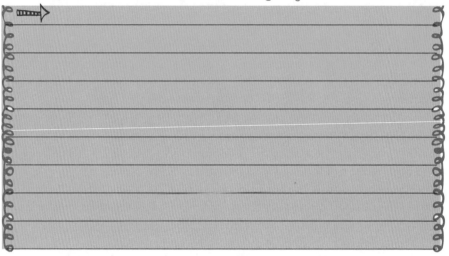

 Tough Stuff

Ready to rip off the Band-Aid? Here are three passages you might find difficult to digest once you bite into God's plan for your design.

> ★ Then the Lord God said, "It is not good that the man should be alone; I will make a helper fit for him." Genesis 2:18

Women were made to be helpers to men. Wives are asked to submit to their husbands. Women are not men's authority. In other words, we are not in charge.

These are the verses that get twisted into a caricature of girlhood that isn't very appealing. As a result, these may be elements of your design that are hard to commit to or even accept.

✿ Truth Is Your Fairy-tale Castle

I hope you read *My Name Is Erin: One Girl's Journey to Discover Truth* because in it I shared that God's Truth is like a fairy-tale castle. Here's what I wrote:

Amusement-park goers often experience something called "museum feet." It's a general feeling of being lost or exhausted that comes from hanging out in such a large space. Having museum feet could give Disney fans a bad experience or cause them to give up and leave the park, but if architects included a large visual landmark such as Cinderella Castle (or the Spaceship Earth at Epcot Center or Hogwarts Castle at Universal Studios' Harry Potter attraction), park goers are less likely to become overwhelmed.

Truth works the same way. Life is big. It is easy to feel lost or overwhelmed or like you want off the ride, but when we know God's Truth, we are anchored and protected from the feeling of "museum feet." Truth gives us a point to come back to when we feel alone, small, or afraid.[18]

The verses about helping and submitting to God's authority structure may overwhelm you at first, but if you continue to study God's Word you'll discover that God's design is hopeful and reassuring.

Let me to encourage you to avoid treating God's Word like a buffet, where you can pick and choose what you like and leave the rest. Instead, embrace it like a gourmet, seven-course meal (yum!). Each flavor enhances the next. Each course contributes to making the whole meal spectacular.

These verses hold complex truths. There is danger in oversimplifying them. Eve was created to be a helper to Adam. We have been assigned the unique role of helpers, and that looks different in each girl's life. For now, you may be a helper to your parents, your siblings, or the single mom next door. Later, you may be a helper to a husband.

Speaking of husbands, that passage from Ephesians says that after you say "I do" to the man God may have for you, your role is to submit to his authority. There's that s-word again . . . *submit*. That doesn't mean you will be like Cinderella in her stepmother's home. You don't have to vow never to express another opinion after your wedding ceremony. A strong marriage needs the wisdom and teamwork of both the bride and the groom. But men and women do have different roles to play in the home. For now, you can live out the heartbeat of those passages by submitting to God's authority and by submitting to the leadership of your dad and praying that, if God's plans for you include marriage, He will bring you a man who will love you "as Christ loved the church."

To read about girls your age who are doing BIG things for God's kingdom, be sure to pick up the next book in this series, My Name Is Erin: One Girl's Mission to Make a Difference.

First Timothy 2:12 says that women are not to teach or exercise authority over a man in church. Men are best equipped to disciple a congregation in the pastoral role. However, this does not mean that you can only do boring, little jobs in your church. Teach a group of girls younger than you. Get involved in raising funds for missions. Play an instrument or sing in a worship service. Feed meals to the homeless. Pray for those who are persecuted around the globe. Organize outreach events. The possibilities are endless and exciting!

We tend to get tripped up on the second part of the passage from 1 Timothy, which says we must be quiet. This verse was written from Paul to Timothy, a young pastor leading one of the early churches. True, Paul and Timothy lived during a different time, when the "rules" and expectations for women were, well, different. But God's intended design for women still applies to today's society and culture.

What about that quiet business? Is God's intention that you would never utter a word in church? Is being quiet a sign that you're God's kind of girl?

I like how author Mary Kassian puts it:

So does God expect us to shut our mouths and never say anything? Are we not allowed to express our opinions? Or discuss, deliberate, or disagree? Does godly womanhood mean we get out the duct tape and slap an "x" over our mouths? That we mutely nod our heads up and down like bobble-head dolls?

When the Bible talks about quietness, it's not referring to an absence of verbal noise as much as it's referring to an absence of spiritual noise. Although there's a connection, quietness has more to do with the state of our hearts than the quantity and volume of our words. Quiet describes a mindset of calmness, serenity and tranquility. It's being settled, steadfast, and peaceful. A quiet disposition is like a still, peaceful pool of water, as opposed to a churning, agitated whirlpool. A quiet spirit is the opposite of an anxious, distressed, disorderly, and clamorous one.[19]

A friend named Marcia wrote to me recently and put it this way:

I believe that when God states a gentle and quiet spirit is of value in His eyes, He is not meaning *quiet* in the sense the world thinks of quiet. God is instead meaning *quiet* as in not causing noise/chaos in our lives and those around us. This noise can be caused by gossiping, fighting, swearing, and encouraging others to fight . . . I am a very outspoken/non-shy woman. God made me that way. It isn't sinful or wrong for me to be this way, as long as I'm using my words to build others up and not to tear them down, thus creating "noise"/chaos in others' lives.

Atta girl, Marcia! You got it.

Not sure when to talk and when to zip those lips?

Here's a great policy to help you choose your words wisely: "Let no corrupting talk come out of your mouths, but only such as is good for building up, as fits the occasion, that it may give grace to those who hear" (Ephesians 4:29).

I told you I don't have all the answers. I'm not a doctor who can write you a prescription for exactly how these Truths will look in your own life. But I do know that God's Word is true and that living out His design is a blessing, not a curse.

"Every word of God proves true; he is a shield to those who take refuge in him" (Proverbs 30:5).

God's instructions for you are always for your good and for the good of your relationships.

❀ Here Comes Trouble

The trouble comes when people twist what God has said. The Bible never says that men are to dominate women in ways that are cruel, oppressive, or abusive. In fact, the Bible says the opposite! There is no excuse for making women feel less than important or lovable. Undervaluing women is not a part of God's design.

Here's a quick and painful tour around the globe. In Kyrgyzstan women are often kidnapped and forced to marry men they did not choose.[20] In India women die in "honor killings," murders carried out by family members when a woman is thought to bring dishonor to her family. As many as 5,000 women and girls are killed this way every year.[21] In China female infants are left to die in dumpsters because girl babies are undervalued.[22] Around the world, nearly two million girls are forced into prostitution as children.[23] Women perform 66 percent of the world's work, produce 50 percent of the food, but earn 10 percent of the income and own 1 percent of the property.[24]

I'm not listing this information for shock value here. I intentionally chose the least graphic examples of oppression, abuse, and undervalued women I could find. My own stomach tied up in knots as I researched the obstacles women face and I realized this isn't just a global problem. You don't have to hop a plane to find women who are treated badly, written off, or made to feel like second-class citizens.

But this is not God's design.

God's didn't create women to be forced into the sex trade. He doesn't ask us to submit just so that men can rule over us. His goal is not to silence women who are desperately crying out for help.

Closer to home, He didn't make you to repress your spiritual gifts, to stop thinking for yourself, to take a vow of silence, or to live under the thumb of mean and demanding men. None of that keeps time with the heartbeat of God.

God loves women! Remember Eve? She reminds us that He made us to be a treasured counterpart and to tell a unique story about Him.

Throughout all the teaching and stories in the entire Bible, God uses women to do really cool things. Jochebed, Moses's mother, made sure Moses was safe enough to become a deliverer of his people someday. Deborah led an army against Israel's enemy—and won! God chose Esther to deliver His people from an oppressive ruler. Rahab helped the Israelites, who were supposed to be her enemies, reach the Promised Land. Mary mothered Jesus. Anna was one of the very few people who recognized the Savior had come. Mary Magdalene was the first person to see Jesus after the resurrection; Jesus chose her to be the first one to tell the disciples He had risen.

Get this: Being a godly girl may be tough, but that just means that it isn't for wimps. It may be difficult to exchange your ways for God's ways, but that's not the same as screaming, "Step on me, please." God has a big mission for you, girl, and it starts with living out His design.

God's girls love to help. They let their own voices get quiet enough to hear the still small voice of God as often as possible. They submit to the authorities God has placed over them because they recognize it is for their good.

✿ Five Ways to Save the Girls

Here are five ways you can get involved in supporting humane treatment of girls in your neighborhood and around the globe.

1 Be Choosy about Chocolate

The chocolate industry is one of the leading contributors to child slavery. Girls and women around the globe are enslaved and forced to work for cocoa farmers and chocolate manufacturers.[25] Look for a Fair Trade or Rainforest Alliance symbol on the packaging of your chocolate bar the next time a craving hits. Better yet, purchase slave-free chocolate and attach it to a card asking others to pray for the girls and women enslaved in the chocolate industry, and then circulate the chocolate among friends and family.

2 Have a Jewelry Party

The organization She Is Safe offers a chance for girls to get involved in helping women simply by shopping with friends. They will send you jewelry handmade by women refugees. You set up a party with your friends so they can shop and watch a video about women in need. The money raised goes to help needy women. Learn more at sheissafe.org.

Chalk Up Awareness

Raise awareness of the dangers women are facing by writing facts about women's issues in sidewalk chalk around your community. Here are a few to get you started.

★ There are sixty million child brides around the world.[26]

★ One in four women will experience domestic violence in her lifetime.[27]

★ The average age of a trafficked girl in the U.S. is thirteen.[28]

Adopt a Truck Stop

Right in our own backyards, truck stops are fast becoming hubs where girls are bought and sold as part of the American trafficking industry. Because of this, it likely is not safe for you to go by yourself to truck stops to pray, but you can adopt a truck stop with your family or youth group and commit to pray for that spot to be a place where girls are rescued, traffickers are stopped, and God's Truth shines.

Consider organizing regular prayer walks at a truck stop in your community. Cry out for God to intervene in the lives of girls who are missing, captive, or on the run.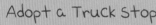

5 Become a Fund-Raiser

There are many organizations working hard to ensure that women are valued, safe, and taken care of, but they need funds to grease the wheels of change. You don't have to have a fat savings account or a high-paying job to help. Come up with creative ways to raise funds and then pass them along to the organizations putting boots on the ground in areas where girls are oppressed. Ask family and friends to sponsor a run, host a chili supper, or roll out a car wash. Then ask God to use those funds to make sure His girls are valued by others.

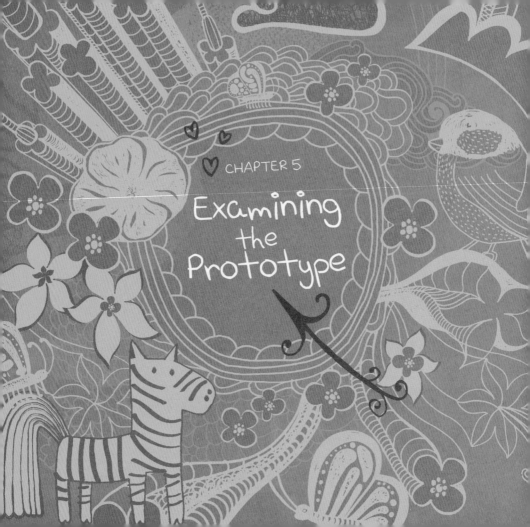

CHAPTER 5

Examining
the
Prototype

It's true that godly girlhood doesn't work like the quadratic formula. You can't plug in this quality plus that quality and get a version of you that perfectly puts God on display. But that doesn't mean there's no common ground among us. We are not identical cardboard cutouts churned out on some massive assembly line, but there are pieces of our design that God intends to unite into a symphony of voices singing praise to Him.

A good way to study God's blueprint for girls is to examine His original design. Eve is the prototype for womanhood after all. She's the very first girl ever given the opportunity to bear the image of God.

Eve: The Life-Giver

You've already read a lot about Eve in this book. That's because she has a lot to show us about God's plan for what it means to be a girl! One characteristic of Eve we can't ignore is that she is a life-giver.

Genesis 3:20 says, "The man called his wife's name Eve, because she was the mother of all living." Eve's name actually means *life-giver*. All humankind would come from her. In that way she is the mother of us all.

"Here we are, Mrs. Beaver, I've found them. Here are the sons and Daughters of Adam and Eve." (Mr. Beaver in The Lion, The Witch and the Wardrobe)

63

I do understand that baby business may not exactly be on your mind. If the idea of maternity pants and contractions makes you squirm a bit, I get it. I do. But you've got to admit that it's pretty cool that God has given us girls the unique ability to carry and bring forth life. The fact that God has created a space in your body to create, nurture, and birth a real-life baby is amazing! I do understand that guys have a role to play, but most of what is required to give life happens with *us*.

But life-giving is not really about us. It's about showing off something about God.

God is the original life-giver. All life is created by Him and through Him: "In the beginning was the Word, and the Word was with God, and the Word was God. He was in the beginning with God. All things were made through him, and without him was not anything made that was made. *In him was life, and the life was the light of men*" John 1:1–4 (emphasis added).

Prototype takeaway:
As a godly girl, I am called to be a life-giver.

When you embrace your God-given role to give life, in His timing, you are showing off one of the most amazing qualities of God. When you choose to speak life-giving words and nurture the life that is already around you, you live out one of the best qualities of Eve. A girl who reflects God well gives life to those around her. There are lots of ways you can live as a life-giver, but let's talk about three, for now.

Speak life-giving words.

Proverbs 18:21 says, "Death and life are in the power of the tongue, and those who love it will eat its fruits." It doesn't matter if you're a thirty-something girl living in the Midwest (that's me!) or a fifteen-year-old girl in the far-off reaches of the globe, your words have the power to tear down those around you or to breathe life into them.

Eve was a life-giver. This part of her design was woven into her very name. You can model the prototype by vowing to speak only life-giving words.

Care for little ones.

You don't have to be a momma to nurture life. You don't have to be pushing a stroller to live like a life-giver. Find ways to care for the littlest ones around you. Teach a Sunday school class. Play catch with your little brother. Offer to volunteer once a week for a stressed-out young mother. Sponsor an impoverished child in an emerging nation. Use some of your money to send gifts through Operation Christmas Child (find out more at samaritanspurse. org). Host a backyard Bible club for the kids in your neighborhood.

The possibilities are endless. Pick a kiddo and look for ways to show him/her God's love. Bingo! You're a life-giver. How very Eve of you.

Be open to motherhood in God's timing.
"First comes love. Then comes marriage. Then comes a big fat paycheck."

Doesn't quite have the right ring to it, does it? I told you earlier in this book that researchers say that fewer and fewer of you want to be mothers. If that's true of you, I know how you feel. I spent my teen years convinced that being a mother was somehow beneath me.

Don't hear me saying that education is bad or having a career is bad. I happen to have both. But don't miss this key point about the prototype of Eve. Being a mother is a high and holy calling. It was a key part of who Eve was made to be and among the very best parts of her life story.

Mothering may be countercultural, but let me encourage you to start praying that God would show you His heart for family.

🌼 Eve: The Helper

Genesis 2:18 says, "Then the Lord God said, 'It is not good that the man should be alone; I will make a *helper* fit for him'" (emphasis added).

Again in Genesis 2:20 we read, "The man gave names to all the livestock and to the birds of the heavens and to every beast of the field. But for Adam there was not found a helper for him".

Eve had many unique roles to play; among them was that she was designed to be a helper to Adam. Being a "helper" isn't usually a valued position. Most of us would rather be the one being helped! But Eve is the first one to show us that being a willing helper is beautiful. In doing so, she was putting a quality of God on display.

Matthew 20:28 is referring to Jesus when it says, "Even as the Son of Man came not to be served but to serve, and to give his life as a ransom for many."

In fact, Eve and Jesus are in cahoots, encouraging you to help others. You can put God on display by cheerfully helping others often: "As each has received a gift, use it to serve one another, as good stewards of God's varied grace" (1 Peter 4:10).

 Keeping It Real

We shouldn't examine the prototype because Eve was the perfect woman. As we all know very well, she was not perfect!. But there is much to learn even from her mistakes. Eve was the first person ever to sin. That sin is recorded in Genesis 3 and is often referred to as "the fall."

Before we go any further, grab your Bible. Quickly read Genesis 3. Jot down anything that stands out to you about the fall in the space below.

> **Prototype takeaway:**
> As a godly girl, I should go out of my way to help others.

_____

_____

_____

_____

_____

_____ ♥

For learning's sake, let's break the fall down into four phases.

 ## Phase 1: The Temptation

Several things stand out to me about Eve's cooperation with the serpent in this story. First, in Genesis 3 we find Eve getting sucked in to a conversation with the serpent because she was so wordy: "And the woman said to the serpent, 'We may eat of the fruit of the trees in this garden, but God said, "You shall not eat of the fruit of the tree that is in the midst of the garden, neither shall you touch it, lest you die"'" Genesis 3:2–3.

You'll have to hit rewind to see Eve's mistake here.

In Genesis 2:16 we read, "And the Lord God commanded man, saying 'You may eat of every tree of the garden, but of the tree of the knowledge of good and evil you shall not eat, for in the day that you eat of it you shall surely die.'"

Did you catch it? God said they could not eat of the tree. Eve said they could not eat of the tree *or* touch it. She was embellishing a bit. Exaggerating. Eve might just have been keeping the conversation going. But she talked too much, she talked too long, and it landed her in a world of hurt.

Do you remember what we learned from Mary's story? Maybe not. Let me give you a refresher. Mary (sister of Martha) loved

Prototype takeaway:
As a godly girl, I will use my words wisely.

to talk to Jesus, and Jesus loved to talk back. So we learn from Mary and Jesus that talking is not a bad thing. Being a godly girl doesn't mean turning in your gift of gab for a vow of silence, but beware the trap of talking just to talk. Eve reminds us of the power of our words.

Prototype takeaway:
As a godly girl, I will find my security in who God made me to be.

There are more lessons to learn from the fall of Eve. In verse 5 the serpent promised that when Eve ate of the tree she would be "like God." In other words, who she was already was not quite enough. Eve fell for it because she was insecure.

Unfortunately, insecurity seems to have become a part of the fabric of every girl. It rarely works in our favor. Had Eve been secure in who she was and how God made her, she might have been less tempted to strive for something more.

In verse 6, Eve is drawn to an element of the fruit that any girl would love: "So when the woman saw that the tree was good for food, *and that it was a delight to the eyes*" (emphasis added). Eve liked pretty things. She was drawn to the fruit because it was a "delight to the eyes." Perhaps it even sparkled a bit in the garden light.

Oh, Eve. I am so much like you!

We girls love our purses, our fashion, and our bling. There's nothing wrong with that. But when we start chasing pretty things (or trying too

69

Prototype
takeaway:
As a godly girl, I will
acknowledge that
pretty things are
not my treasure.

hard to *be* the pretty thing!), when pretty things dictate our decisions, when they occupy too much of our time and money and thoughts, we get tripped up just like Eve did.

The next phase of the fall shows us what the stakes are.

 Phase 2: The Nibble

Genesis 3:6 describes the fatal moment: "So when the woman saw that the tree was good for food, and that it was a delight to the eyes, and that the tree was to be desired to make one wise, she took of its fruit and ate, and she also gave some to her husband who was with her, and he ate" (Genesis 3:6).

When Eve sinned, she took others down in her wake. Certainly Adam was a willing participant. Eve did not force-feed him the forbidden fruit. But notice that Eve was not the only person affected by her sin.

The same is true for all daughters of Eve. Our sin affects those around us.

Sin isn't fun to think about. The effects of sin leave an even more bitter taste in our mouths, but the danger of sin is yet

Prototype
takeaway:
As a godly girl, I will
recognize that my
sin has consequences
for me and for
those I love.

another reason why a godly girl is a student of God's Word. She is a seeker of God's heart and a warrior who fights against the temptation to sin.

"I have stored up your word in my heart, that I may not sin against you" (Psalm 119:11).

Phase 3: The Cover-Up

As soon as Eve sinned, she went into fix-it mode: Genesis 3:7 describes how she and Adam sewed fig leaves together to cover themselves. Verse 8 tells how they hid from God. Verse 13 shows Eve deflecting the blame onto the serpent. We never see Eve accept responsibility for her sin.

We girls tend to be fix-ers. We try to fix people, fix problems, fix situations. But the only one who could fix Eve's problems is the same One who can fix ours. Let Eve teach you to run to God when you're in a mess.

Eve also deflected blame as she pointed the finger at others instead of accepting responsibility for her own actions. Deflecting isn't a girl characteristic; it's a human characteristic. But it's not

Prototype takeaway:
As a godly girl, I will seek God's help instead of trying to fix everything myself.

good for anyone, boys or girls. This is one area where we must choose *not* to live like Eve. Don't point your fingers. Don't place blame. Break out of Eve's mold by acknowledging your tendency to sin and depending heavily on your Maker to reshape you.

> Prototype takeaway: I will acknowledge my sin and ask my Maker to make me more like Him.

 ## Phase 4: The Maker Responds

What does God do in the aftermath of Eve's sin? Surely His heart was broken by her choices. This was not His plan. Think of Him again like a Potter. His creation had fallen off the Potter's wheel. She hadn't stayed in the shape He intended her to. His masterpiece was cracked.

What would most potters do at this point? They'd throw the broken pieces into the scrap pile, flatten the clay down, and start over. They would give up on a work of art gone wrong.

But that is not what the Potter did. God does not throw Eve aside. From the very first girl we learn that God doesn't intend for girls to be tossed out, undervalued, or treated as second-class citizens.

God did hand down punishment, but then He lovingly made garments and clothed Adam and Eve (Genesis 3:21). He didn't sentence them to instant death but instead sent them out beyond the walls of the garden where they lived long and fruitful lives.

🌸 A Godly Girl Send-Off

You may or may not have lived like a godly girl up to this point—and you won't do it perfectly after you close this book. But you can rest in knowing that God is not a God who tosses girls aside. He is not a Potter who throws broken creations in the scrap pile. He is willing and able to keep you on the Potter's wheel and to shape you to look like the girl He made you to be.

With that in mind, I join Eve, Hannah, Mary, Martha, and the Gallery in commissioning you to embrace your God-given design. We send you out to be the girls God made you to be. I imagine you like an army of mirrors of all shapes and sizes, in big cities and small towns, united by these shared goals—to put God on display, to seek His heart for what it means to be a girl, and to willingly live as He calls you to live.

We may not all be girly girls, but we will seek to be godly girls because God is worth reflecting.

We are the daughters of Eve. We are the workmanship of a loving God. We are the mirrors He wants to use to reflect His love.

This is our story.

Notes

1. Susan Donaldson James, "Baby Storm Raised Genderless Is Bad Experiment, Says Experts," *Good Morning America*, May 26, 2011. http://abcnews.go.com.

2. Associated Press, "Sealed with a (Lesbian) Kiss: Gay Sailors Share Navy's Traditional Homecoming Embrace as Ship Returns," MailOnline, December 23, 2011. www.dailymail.co.uk.

3. Daily Mail reporter, "You're All Equal Here: Swedish School Bans 'Him' and 'Her' in Bid to Stop Children Falling into Gender Stereotypes," MailOnline, June 27, 2011. www.dailymail.co.uk.

4. National Public Radio, "'Mental Hygiene' Films: Lost and Found Sound: School Movies Learned for Social Education," *All Things Considered,* National Public Radio, November 12, 1999. www.npr.org.

5. American Experience, "People & Events: Mrs. America: Women's Roles in the 1950s," *The Pill,* American Experience, 1999–2001. www.pbs.org.

6. Linda Napikoski, "1960s Feminist Activities: What Did Feminists Do During the 1960s?" *Women's History,* About.com, accessed November 20, 2012. http://womenshistory.about.com.

7. Pauline Weston Thomas, "Power Dressing: 1980s Fashion History," Fashion-Era, accessed November 20, 2012. www.fashion-era.com.

8. W. Bradford Wilcox, "When Marriage Disappears: The Retreat from Marriage in Middle America," *The 2010 State of Our Unions* report, December 2010. http://stateofourunions.org.

9. Ellen Galinsky, Kerstin Aumann, and James T. Bond, "Times Are Changing: Gender and Generation at Work and at Home," Families and Work Institute, August 2011. www.familiesandwork.org.

10. Barna Group, "Top Trends of 2011: Women Making it Alone," Barna Group, accessed November 20, 2012. www.barna.org.

11. Wilcox, "When Marriage Disappears."

12. Nancy Leigh DeMoss and Dannah Gresh, *Lies Young Women Believe: And the Truth That Sets Them Free* (Chicago: Moody Publishers, 2008), 162.

13. Rodgers and Hammerstein, "I Enjoy Being a Girl," from the musical *Flower Drum Song,* 1958.

14. Katherine Rosman, "Read It and Weep, Crybabies," *The Wall Street Journal,* May 4, 2011. http://online.wsj.com.

15. Ibid.

16. Fiona Macrae, "Women Talk Three Times as Much as Men, Says Study," accessed November 8, 2012, http://www.dailymail.co.uk/femail/article-419040/Women-talk-times-men-says-study.html.

17. Ibid.

18. Erin Davis, *My Name Is Erin: One Girl's Journey to Discover Truth* (Chicago: Moody Publishers, 2013), 38–39.

19. Mary Kassian, "Give Me a Quiet Mind," Girls Gone Wise blog, June 18, 2011. www.girlsgonewise.com.

20. Rushfan, "7 Terrible Abuses Suffered by Women around the World," Listverse, June 10, 2008. http://listverse.com.

21. Ibid.

22. Mark Litke, "Some Chinese Leaving Baby Girls for Dead," *ABC News,* August 25, 2012. http://abcnews.go.com.

23. She Is Safe, "Child Prostitution," accessed November 21, 2012. http://sheissafe.org.

24. She Is Safe, "Oppression," accessed November 21, 2012. http://sheissafe.org.

25. Eatocracy, "The Bitter Truth behind the Chocolate in Your Easter Basket," April 4, 2012. http://eatocracy.cnn.com.

26. CARE, "Help End Child Marriage," accessed November 21, 2012. www.care.org.

27. Domestic Violence Resource Center, "Domestic Violence Statistics," accessed November 21, 2012. www.dvrc-or.org.

28. International Crisis Aid, "Sex Trafficking in the United States," accessed November 21, 2012. www.crisisaid.org.

Acknowledgments

My momma taught me better than to receive a gift without sending a thank-you note. This series is the end result of many gifts—people who love me well, friends who cheer me on, and fellow Jesus-lovers who consistently point me toward God's Truth. If you fit into one (or all) of those three camps, this page is my thank-you note to you. (Be sure to mention to my mom that I sent it!)

The Gab Gallery. I loved the girls I met during the research phase of this book. Your openness and honesty helped me know what to write. You also encouraged and inspired me by proving my suspicions that God is using young women to do big things. Keep letting Him use you. I'm on the edge of my seat waiting to see what mountains God will move with your generation. I did not get to meet all of you personally; instead some of you had the treat of hanging out with my friend Dree. Speaking of . . .

Dree. Dree was my focus-group leader for the book. She hung out with girls in places like Little Rock, Springfield, and Tulsa. Anyone who had the chance to spend time with Dree knows what a treasure she is. Dree, I credit you with giving me the Truth bug. Your passion for God and His Word is positively infectious. Thanks for consistently pressing me to choose God's Truth and to live my life according to His Word. If we were back in junior high, I'd want you to wear the other half of my BFF necklace.

Holly, René, and Team Moody. I am so thankful for a publishing team who believes in the message of God's Truth and entrusts me to deliver that message to young women. Your kindness bowls me over. Thank you.

Jason, Eli, and Noble. At the end of the day, I am Jason's wife and Eli's and Noble's mom. These are the roles that bring me the most joy and force me to keep running to God's Word for answers. My sweet family listened to endless readings as this work evolved from an idea into a four-book series. When the process got stressful, they did things like make me a leaf pile and invite me to jump in. Family, I adore you. You are the very best part of my story.

Jesus. Thank You, Jesus, for being so completely irresistible.

Also available as ebooks

MOODY
PUBLISHERS

978-0-8024-0644-6   978-0-8024-0642-2   www.MoodyPublishers.com   978-0-8024-0643-9   978-0-8024-0643-9